The Mermaid and the Centaur

By Tamuna Tsertsvadze and Tiegan Brown

D1532474

The Mermaid and the Centaur

***

Legend tells us, that in the beautiful Black Sea, in deep past, there existed a rich kingdom, where lived the mermen and the mermaids – sea creatures with a human body and a fish tail. They had cities and a king whose castle was located in the capital, built of marbles, gold, and silver. The king had three daughters: Morena, the eldest one, whom he gave to the prince of the Marmara Sea; the middle one, Irina, whom he gave to the prince of the Azov Sea; and the little one, Coralia, whom he planned to give to the great prince of the Mediterranean Sea.

The kingdoms were in peace with each other, but who knew, that it wouldn't last for long? In the depths of the sea, there lived a black mage, Deitis, who controlled a terrible beast of the deep waters. Deitis was angry since they didn't give a single princess to him, so he craved for vengeance...

Coralia was in her room as usual, combing her hair and talking to her staunch dolphin, Morey.

"Oh, Morey, I so greatly dislike that prince of the Mediterranean Sea! He's disgusting!"

Morey just giggled, as dolphins usually do.

"Why does father have to make me marry that man? I should be able to choose one for myself!"

Morey swam up to her and nudged her softly to try to make her feel better. A servant swam in and reported:

"Your highness, the king and all the other nobles are calling for you. The majestic prince of the Mediterranean will soon be here".

She swam out. Coralia sighed, for she was very sad that her marriage was getting closer and closer. Suddenly, she heard a terrible shriek from below. She got horrified and looked out the window –a huge fish-like beast with big teeth had attacked the castle! It had stormed in through the underwater palace, as if looking for something. It growled terribly, its eyes glowing yellow. Coralia backed away from the window and cuddled with Morey. They were both terrified, wondering what would happen.

The beast looked through the window with his terrible yellow eyes, and roared. He broke the window with his fin, grabbed shrieking

Coralia and swam away from the castle, leaving it broken and miserable. The king screamed once saw his daughter in the terrible beast's fins:

"No, Coralia!"

But it was too late, for the beast with Coralia was gone. King Marinus fell to his knees, crying for his daughter...

Coralia woke up. She felt dizzy. She found herself tied in a purple coral room, where there was a big purple sphere put on the pedestal. There was pink smoke inside the sphere.

A tall man with long black hair and light-blue eyes came out of the dark. He was wearing a black cloak on his black clothes. He grinned.

"Hello, princess," a deep, sly voice sounded from his lips. The princess averted her gaze from him. "Look at me when I'm talking to you!" the man frowned and grabbed her cheek with his light-blue-finned hand, making her look at him. She shivered at his cold touch. Her shimmering light grey eyes stared at him. He smiled: "You really are a beauty, princess..."

Tear streamed down Coralia's cheeks. She closed her eyes, quivering:

"Let me go! Please..."

The man laughed evilly:

"Let you go? Why, when I can marry you and become the ruler of the Black Sea? Oh, that is what I will do!"

Coralia shoved him away:

"No, I will not allow you to marry me, you horrible man!"

Deitis grew furious:

"Princess, I warn you – I can destroy you with my scaly hands".

"Go away!"

"Very well! Then say goodbye to your precious kingdom..." He whistled. The same terrible beast Coralia had seen in her kingdom entered. The mermaid princess screamed. The beast gave out a horrendous growl. The mage grinned: "My boy, go and bring me King Marinus of the Black Sea!"

The beast snarled and swam out. Tears poured from Coralia's eyes:

"No, please!"

The mage laughed hideously:

"Now I will capture your father and become the sole ruler of the Black Sea!"

Coralia watched in dread how the terrible beast went to put an end to her kingdom...

The beast arrived at the palace. King Marinus was still sitting miserably on his throne when he heard the loud monster again. He ordered his daughters to hide, in fear that they would be taken too. He took his trident and called for all the mermen knights to mount their huge sea-horses and fight the beast.

He led the army himself. They attacked the beast and stabbed him with their trident and spears, but there was no single scratch marked on the terrible creature. Marinus widened eyes, for he had never seen such a thing before. The beast only became more aggressive when they tried to attack him and ate one of the knights up. The others swam away in fear, but Marinus did not – he had instead frozen in shock.

The beast grabbed the king and swam away. He brought the prisoner to the mage. This latter laughed evilly and chained him up.

"Now you both are mine," he eyed the princess and the king, "Die here before I get to rule your kingdom!"

He sat on the beast and swam away. The king sighed:

"It's over, we all are doomed. Oh, Great Poseidon, why did you bring such a misfortune upon us, what have we done to you? Oh... oh..."

Meanwhile, the mage arrived at the castle.

"Bow down to me, you miserable beings, for I am your new leader!"

He blasted deadly purple rays out of his purple staff. The mermaids all across the kingdom stopped what they were doing and stood before him bowing down, terrified by the appearance of the beast and the rage of the mage. This latter took a seat on the throne and let out a hideous laugh:

"Very good! From now on, you all are my slaves! The mermen will hunt for my beast, if not, he will eat *you*, and the mermaids will dance to amuse me!"

Thus, the mermen and the mermaids of the Black Sea became slaves of the evil mage and his terrible beast. Such was their horrible fate...

***

In the forbidden waters, away from the kingdom, there was another mermaid hanging out in her usual spot – Loreley, a lonely mermaid, for she had never really had any friends.

One day, when Loreley was swimming in forbidden waters as usual, she spotted a little merman swimming through water-plants, armed with a spear, looking for some fish to kill. The mermaid got surprised, for no merman had ever hit these forbidden waters before – they believed there were ghosts of the dead wandering out there. Yet, this little merman was here, so it astonished her. She approached him, wanting to talk, but once the merman saw her, he cried and hid within water-plants. Loreley crept closer as she was curious about who he was. The merman hid deeper into the plants.

"I'm not going to hurt you. I'm all alone too..."

The little merman, encouraged by Loreley's words, came out of the plants and cast his eyes down.

"I'm not alone. I have a family... I mean, three sisters, and a whole kingdom. We're under an evil mage's control – the one who makes the mermen feed his terrible beast and the mermaids amuse him by their dance. If we don't obey him, he threatens us to give us to his beast as food!"

The little merman started crying. Loreley began to pity him so she wondered which kingdom he was talking about. The only one close-by was her home... Finally, she decided to ask him:

"Where's your kingdom?"

"The kingdom of the Black Sea," answered the little merman, "I'm the Black Sea prince, Sean".

Loreley was shocked – it was her home, her mother was still there! She fell into thoughts. She needed to save her and Sean's people, but how? – The wizards of the sea were powerful. Only the god could come up with an idea of how to defeat them, only the god knew their weak spots. The god... Yes, Poseidon!

"Listen," she turned to Sean, "Let's go to Great Poseidon's palace and tell him everything. Maybe he will be able to help us".

Sean brightened:

"Yes, he's our only hope!"

They swam to the god's dwelling together. Poseidon lived in an enormous marble palace in the centre of the Mediterranean Sea. He was sitting on the golden throne, holding his trident and thinking about the ungrateful humans sailing above his seas and not giving him gifts for letting them sail peacefully. At this time, Loreley and Sean entered and bowed before him, showing their respect and awe.

"What has brought you here, my children?" Poseidon asked with a sweet and kind voice of an all-father.

Loreley replied shyly:

"Sir... our kingdom is being taken over by a powerful mage. Please, help us!"

"My lord," Sean took up, "please, he rules over us and makes us feed his beast!"

Poseidon grew incensed:

"What? How does Hades dare bring his stupid mages in my seas?! Let all the Mediterranean mermen help you!"

The Mediterranean mermen army gathered and, with the leadership of the Mediterranean prince – Princess Coralia's fiancé – went to the Black Sea to fight the mage and his beast. Loreley and Sean were determined to save their kingdom, so they joined in the battle too.

The mage let his beast fight the mermen. The mermen struck spears at him, but no scratch could be marked on his body. The terrible beast growled in rage and ate some of the mermen. The others muddled and swam away. The creature swam after the Mediterranean prince and swallowed him too. The mage laughed evilly:

"Even your stupid leader couldn't beat my boy! You all are miserable! Hahaha!"

Loreley tried to think of a way to kill the merciless beast and decided stabbing him in the heart might be the best way... but how could that be achieved?

"We need to call those who are fishing on the huge beasts like this!" Sean cried, "We need creatures from above the sea!"

An idea struck Loreley's mind:

"Let's go ask Poseidon to turn us into humans, and search for our helpers above the sea!"

Sean agreed. They went back to Poseidon and asked him to turn them temporarily into humans. Their wish was fulfilled. Loreley and Sean went up on the surface. They had feet now, instead of tails.

"How can we move with these?" Sean looked at his feet. He barely stood up, stumbled and fell down. "Damn!"

Loreley too, was having trouble standing up.

"I know, right! How do humans even do this?"

Luckily for them, a human was walking nearby and noticed them stumbling on the beach.

"Hey, are you guys okay?"

Sean got scared:

"Keep quiet, he has noticed us!"

He immediately hushed up and took a seat on the beach, but Loreley didn't want to keep quiet – she knew they needed help.

"We're a merman and a mermaid!" she cried to the human, "We got human forms from Poseidon, to get help from above the seas!"

The human cackled:

"A merman and a mermaid? You're kidding me?"

He thought these strange people were playing a prank on him. Loreley got angry:

"Yes, we are. You have to believe me! We need help!"

"Listen guys, the only thing I know is that you're on the centaurs' territory. If you don't get up and run away as soon as possible, there's a hundred percent chance that you will be killed," the human walked off.

"Hey! No! Come back!" cried Sean, but it was late, for the human had already gone. "Ugh, damn it! Now we're truly doomed. Zeus doesn't even care about us to save us!"

Loreley got upset:

"Humans really don't believe we exist".

"Yeah…" Sean sighed.

Suddenly they heard a sound of horses' hooves', as if there was a horse herd somewhere nearby. Strange creatures on the beach – they had horse bodies and feet below, and human bodies and heads above. They saw Loreley and Sean and frowned. One of them, the blond one with a white horse-body, shouted:

"Hey, you there, stupid humans, didn't we tell you not to step in here? You're grounded!"

He took a huge labrys[1]. The other creatures also grabbed their weapons, each of them a different type. Loreley answered:

---

[1] Labrys – a double-headed battle-axe

"We are not humans. I am a mermaid and he is a merman. We have come here to get help!"

The blond centaur burst out laughing:

"A mermaid? A merman? Are you kidding me?" he touched their feet with his hooves: "Hmm, I don't sense a fish tail here!" He laughed along with the whole herd. Then he raised his labrys: "Prepare to die!"

"Tesoros!" a brunet centaur shouted with a frown, "be ashamed! How can you threaten a girl?!" he glanced at Loreley. "Let's take them both to our chief and let him judge them".

"Ugh, okay…"

Tesoros grunted and put his labrys down. The centaurs grabbed Loreley and Sean and took them into the forest. Loreley began to cry:

"We will never save our kingdom like this! Everyone thinks we are lying".

"Don't worry…" Sean tried to calm her down, even though he was no less concerned.

They arrived at a cave. The centaurs went in. There was a tall, pitch-black-horse-bodied centaur sitting on the bear skins. He had a tan human skin, oblong fire-coloured hair, and expressive, wise light-blue eyes. He wore a golden crown on the head. The herd bowed before him.

"These humans were on our beach," Tesoros pointed him on Loreley and Sean, "Kind Lisandros told me not to kill them and bring them to you," he cackled as he glanced at Lisandros – the brunet centaur next to him. "They also claim to be a mermaid and a merman".

The chief observed Loreley and Sean. Then he asked in a calm, strict, but kind voice:

"Why are you here, on the surface?"

"Ugh, finally, someone believes us!" Sean regained his hopes.

Loreley bowed down to the chief:

"We have come to the surface because a mage has taken over our kingdom and we needed help".

The black centaur furrowed his brow:

"Hades… I had a dream, where Zeus told me that the water would need us. It looks like the day has come. Do you have anything to give us, so we could breathe underwater?"

Loreley shyly smiled:

"Well, all mermaids have the power to make anyone breathe underwater".

"Well then, we all are coming. Aren't we, boys? Let us go fishing!"

Tesoros grinned:

"Sure, Chief!"

Loreley and Sean tried to stand up once again but fell. They blushed with embarrassment. The chief chuckled. He grabbed Loreley and put her onto his horseback, while Lisandros took Sean.

They ran to the beach. Sean and Loreley jumped into the water and their feet turned back to fish tails. They gave the centaurs the temporal ability to breathe underwater and were soon joined by them. The centaurs ran deeper and deeper into the water, following the mermaid and the merman, and soon arrived at the Black Sea kingdom. The mage got frightened once saw them:

Oh no, the centaurs! They are wise. They will know how to defeat my beast...

He ordered the beast to eat the centaurs. Tesoros swung his labrys and hit the creature. Oh, miracle, blood poured off his huge wound! The labrys was sharp enough so it was able to cut the creature's body. Now Lisandros swung his sword and caused another heavy wound to the beast. The monster was roaring miserably. Finally, the chief lanced his sharp spear and hit the beast right in the heart. The beast fell down dead.

The mage grew terrified and fled from the scene. The mermen and the mermaids failed to notice him. They happily whooped and thanked the centaurs for saving them. These latter ones accepted their gratitude with gracious smiles. But then, Sean stopped dancing:

"What about my sister and father? They are still missing!"

Now Loreley noticed the mage wasn't there:

"Where has that sorcerer gone?"

The centaurs, Loreley, and Sean began searching around for the mage. Meanwhile, he was hiding in his castle, looking around attentively, scared that they would eventually find him. Indeed, soon the chief of the centaurs sensed the mage's presence.

"I know where he is! Follow me!"

He ran to the direction where the castle was located. They soon arrived there. The mage frowned and came out.

"Well, you have found me, but it's far from over!"

He blasted them with a purple ray. The centaurs dodged. The blast hit Loreley instead, and she bowed down to the mage. This latter grinned:

"I have taken your precious friend!"

Sean got angry and so did the centaurs. They gave a battle cry and attacked him. Lisandros swung his sword and broke the mage's staff! It also broke the spell on Loreley.

"No!"

The mage fell onto his knees holding his precious broken staff. Tesoros cackled:

"It looks like we are the ones to have defeated you!"

He swung his labrys at full strength and killed the mage. There was no more an evil sorcerer to destroy the kingdom. They only had to find King Marinus and Princess Coralia. The chief closed his eyes. He heard a voice:

"They're in the dungeon…"

He quickly reopened the eyes and led the team into the dungeon. He knew it was the voice of Poseidon. The team easily found Marinus and Coralia, chained up to a coral wall. When the centaur chief's and Coralia's gazes met, they froze on the place – those eyes… they were so mysterious and beautiful! Chief Leseus knew immediately that it was his soulmate, and Coralia had likewise guessed she had fallen for this centaur.

Sean ran up to his older sister and hugged her:

"I missed you so much, sister!"

He then untied her while Loreley untied the king. Marinus widened eyes when saw the centaurs had saved their lives.

"Oh my, thanks to Zeus and Poseidon, for sending us these heroes from above!"

"If not for your two brave people," Chief Leseus pointed on Loreley and Sean, "we wouldn't have been informed about your trouble, therefore, wouldn't have come".

Marinus smiled with pride:

"Oh, Sean, good job my boy! And you," he turned to Loreley, "how can I thank you, my child?"

Loreley bowed down to him:

"Sir, you do not have to thank me, I am happy to have saved our kingdom".

Sean smiled at Loreley knowing that she was for sure a hero... but he also felt some sort of attraction towards her. She was so beautiful... So he swam up to his father and told him:

"Father, do you remember when you talked to me about bringing a princess? You told me that the true king needs a queen beside. At that time, I didn't know who my princess would be. I guess, now I do know..."

Loreley realised whom he was talking about and blushed – she had also taken a liking to this handsome prince. Marinus chuckled:

"Well then, does she accept to be your princess?"

Loreley smiled, her cheeks grown all red:

"Of course, I would be happy to be his princess".

They then glanced at Coralia, who had already approached the chief of centaurs and was hugging him. Marinus widened eyes:

"But... but..."

Sean heaved a sigh:

"It is okay, father. The prince of the Mediterranean Sea is dead. The only heir left to the Mediterranean throne is a princess, and they said they're going to marry her to the prince of the Atlantic Ocean".

Marinus, too, sighed at this sorrowful news.

"Well, the centaurs have saved our lives. He may have her... But how will a mermaid be with a centaur and with us at the same time?"

20

Leseus, having overheard their conversation, smiled:

"Your Majesty, I know a way. There exist such creatures on the surface, called amphibians, which can live both on the ground and underwater. If we ask Poseidon to give the same powers to your child, she will be able to live with me and, once she enters water, become a mermaid again and see you".

Marinus brightened up:

"You are very clever, I should say! I guess the rumours about the centaurs' deep wisdom are truthful. Well then, let the princess of the Black Sea be yours!"

"Thank you, Your Majesty!"

Leseus bowed to Marinus as a sign of respect. Coralia grew happy and hugged the king:

"Thank you so much, father!"

"You're welcome, my children. Let you be joyful forever!"

Many months after, Coralia was married to Leseus, while Loreley and Sean became the next king and queen. Coralia could walk on land as a human and swim underwater as a mermaid. Poseidon fulfilled her wish, as he knew she was doing it for true love. Leseus and Coralia were happy together, riding the fields on the surface and swimming through water-plants under the sea.

Such was a legend about a centaur that saved a mermaid and fell in love with her. True love can demolish any obstacles – even bond those two who are completely different creatures, because with their souls, they are one...